yan and the pike

Jun Machida

By the same author:
Christmas in the Steppes
The Pike's Violin

j Japan 2001

This edition has been produced
with the assistance of Japan 2001.
First published in the UK by
acorn book company
PO Box 191
Tadworth
Surrey KT20 5YQ

email: sales@acornbook.co.uk

www.acornbook.co.uk

ISBN 0 9534205 4 X

British Library Cataloguing in Publication Data
A catalogue record for this book is available from the British Library.

Translated from the Japanese by Sophia Poznansky
First published in Japan by Publisher Michitani Co. Ltd, Tokyo
Copyright © Jun Machida, 1997
This translation copyright © acorn book company, 2002

Printed and bound in Great Britain by Biddles Ltd

First printing 2002. Second printing 2003.

For Yan

A note on the author

Author and illustrator Jun Machida was born in Tokyo in 1951.

For many years he ran the Odessa-Istanbul Cafe in Shibuya, where his charming pictures of Yan the cat were first exhibited. These attracted such attention from his customers that he began writing *The Private Papers of Yan*.

And so was born the first in a series of stories: *Yan and the Pike*.

CONTENTS

CONTENTS

Introduction

I like the hour just before dawn. The sound of bird-song carried on the wind reaches me faintly through the crack in the window next to the seat where I am sitting, motionless.

This, is a moment to be treasured.

Without thinking, I go outside and take in the smell of the foliage, carried to me secretly on the quiet dawn breeze. The Caucasian carpets, hanging to dry, scatter the pride of the people, as the smell of the damp sheep's wool is carried away by the wind.

I am not one to be proud of my people, nor particularly attached to my town. I take a look at the fallen leaves, and glimpse the sky between the trunks and branches of the trees that still remain in the little wood. I take it all in without lowering my eyes below the level of the horizon.

How fortunate we would be if one day the industry in this country were to decline and the wind were to blow a little stronger.

The air would become slightly transparent - just as it used to be - and after a while, perhaps, the leaves on the trees would start to shine out with their former green, and the stripes in the bark would rise up clearly to the surface.

At the moment though, it is still dark - and one or two stars are shining. They are a hint that today we shall have a clear sky and white clouds. But for now, it is a colourless, weakly blue and fragile world.

Fortunately the city, still tired perhaps from the fatigue of the day and fed up with its daily life, is silently sleeping away.

The voice of a cricket, plaintively mourning over his own little tragedy, rings out through the night. Rather pitifully, he uses up all his strength and ends up falling fast asleep.

Dimly, both that sound and the deepening blue sky drift away to a strange and distant land.

For some time now my cat, Yan, has been sprawled out on the chair outside. He has opened his pale eyes and is becoming aware of the sound of birds calling from unseen treetops, and the smell of the drying carpets.

He is not really sleeping, nor has he yet woken up. He has just remembered something... and is trying to forget something.

Ah. This is the moment we should treasure...

And yet, in this country, very few people actually experience this moment at all.

The very thing I am trying to draw in my pictures is this moment- the fleeting instant while a thought is forming in the mind. As I begin, the thought lies somewhere between the conscious and the unconscious. It is veiled by a big white cloth, unable to breathe. It flies into the air and then suddenly falls back to earth with a jolt. That is the moment I am trying to catch.

When daybreak comes to this town, it doesn't signify the start of the day, but its end.

When the sky becomes completely light and the town begins to stir, this country enters a deep night - only the imagination could create such a darkness.

I do not draw pictures of my own country or my town, because it is no longer beautiful. There is no hardship or sadness any more, and I can't even find the kind of wide-open grassland that makes my imagination soar.

'Come on,' I say to Yan: 'Let's go to bed.'

To which he gives a short: 'Uhuh.'

And suddenly, as Yan enters sleep, his whole body is bathed in the bright light of the night and he begins to dream...

J.M

Bosphorus
In the twilight

Yan crossing the Bosphorus in the Twilight

yan and the pike

'Knock, knock.' I had the feeling that someone was rather hesitantly knocking at my door but having overdone it a bit on the fish soup, I was finding it rather troublesome to get my body to move, so I just stayed where I was on the bed, rolled over to one side. I was just dozing off again when, once more, there was a cautious: knock, knock knocking.

My hut was on the slope of a low hill. It was situated in a place where nobody lived, overlooking grassland and a little wood spread out like patchwork. Beyond the wood, as if touching the horizon, you could see the long meandering silver river.

I hadn't seen a soul for several months so, thinking that it had probably all been in my imagination, I was just about to forget about the whole thing when, yet again, there came another hesitant 'Knock, knock, knock, knock.'

Reluctantly, I got up and went over to the doorway and opened the door - whose hinges I had just repaired the week before - and there stood a solitary pike.*

'Hello. What super weather we're having today. I seem to have come somewhat further than I planned. Er... I'm a pike. Yes... the one who lives over there in that shining river... Ahem. How do you do? My name is Pike! You see that shining river over there...?'

---

* Pike: a large freshwater fish that lives in clean water. It is dark green in colour and can grow up to one metre long. It has a long life span and it is said that some have lived to be over a hundred years old.

Pike at the door

Of course I was surprised by the fact that my unexpected visitor had turned out to be a pike, but even more than that, struck by the sight of the golden fields glinting in the morning light behind him - and the leaves glistening on the trees in the wood beyond that.

We were already in the midst of autumn.

We chatted together for a little short of an hour. I told him about how I managed to get along living in the grassland, about a wood where you could pick lots of mushrooms and about how to make and keep jam. He told me about how he made a life for himself in the river, about the place to go to find lots of river bugs and about an easy way to swim.

That's how Mr Pike and I became friends.

When it was time to go home he said, rather apologetically: 'Ah yes... erm, tomorrow I will be celebrating my name day* and I have to make some mushroom soup but, er, unfortunately I've completely gone and run out of salt and butter... I'm terribly sorry but, well... you wouldn't have a bit you could lend me, would you?'

'OK,' I said, and I handed him a small bag of salt and some butter wrapped in paper, which I put into a net-mesh bag.

* Name day: in the Russian Orthodox Church, each day of the year is dedicated to a particular saint. There are more than 1,500 saints altogether so some people have the same name day even though they have different names. In pre-Revolutionary times, people celebrated their name days even more than their birthdays.

Swinging the two bags, he slowly went off down the slope.

Pike with his two bags going off down the slope

The next day, having completely forgotten all about the day before, I was fast asleep when there came the sound of a 'Knock, knock,' at the door. I wanted to continue sleeping but seeing as I hadn't eaten that much fish soup the day before, and was beginning to feel hungry again, I thought I might as well get up.

Admiring the hinge that I had just repaired, I opened the door and, once again, Mr Pike was standing there. 'Hello Yan, fine weather we're having again eh? If this good weather lasts, I'll have to go on an outing everyday, which could get rather troublesome. By the way, did you have a good sleep? Ah good, I am glad. As for me, I was busy thinking 'where shall I go tomorrow?' It was so much fun I didn't sleep very well at all. And also...'

Yan and the Pike at the door

I chatted with Mr Pike for a little less than an hour.

I taught him an easy way of opening a jam jar and how to fix the hinges on a door.

He taught me what best to do in the event of drowning in the river and how to use a stone to scrub and shine one's body with.

When it was time to go home he said, rather apologetically: 'Oh, yes, I'm celebrating my name day tomorrow, and was planning to make mushroom soup but unfortunately, I've gone and run clean out of smetana*... Would you mind lending me a little bit?'

'Yeah, okay,' I said and handed him some smetana in a jar, just as it was.

Mr Pike, holding the jar with the smetana in it, slowly descended the autumnal steppe.
Every now and then a gust of wind came along and as the tall grass shook, it looked just like Mr Pike was swimming through the grassland.

* Smetana: Russian sour cream. Used in the preparation of almost all Russian food. At other times it is placed on the table to be put into soup and that sort of thing.

Mr Pike swimming through the grassland

The following morning it was raining. I didn't have anything special to do so I decided to snap off the sprouts that had grown on the potatoes and after that to make some blackcurrant jam.

As the evening drew on the rain let up. The air became cool and one could feel the autumn drawing in. Blue sky spread out rapidly between the gaps in the rain clouds and that made me feel more cheerful.

Just then, there was a faint 'Knock, knock,' sound. 'Ah! That might be Mr Pike,' I thought, whilst opening the door, taking note of the hinge as I did so. And who should I find out there but Mr Pike, standing tall.

'What a downpour that was, wasn't it! When it rains like that, you can't be going anywhere. But how dramatic the sky is when the rain has just stopped. It was so exciting to watch all the different shaped clouds flying past! I was running after a cloud and ended up coming all the way here! By the way, what have you been getting up to, Yan?'

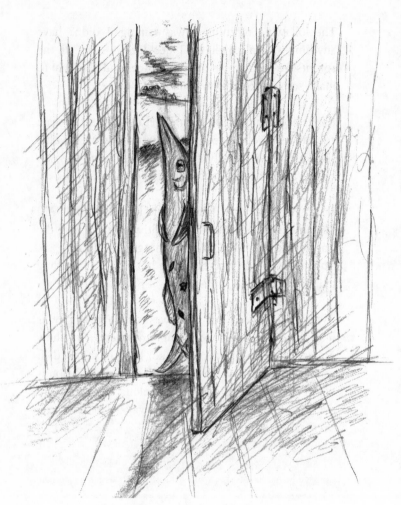

Pike at the door, covered in leaves

There was an assortment of yellow leaves in various shapes and sizes stuck to Mr Pike's body, which had probably attached themselves to him on the way, as he walked along.

And so, like the day before, I ended up talking with Mr Pike for just short of an hour. He told me how the clouds, reflected in the surface of the river, change when the water ripples, and the colour of the river varies depending on the time of day.

I explained to him which herbs were best to use when pickling cucumber and told him points to pay attention to when cooking mushroom pirogi.*

* Pirogi: a kind of big pie-like thing made from various different ingredients and served baked or fried. For example there is cabbage pirogi, meat pirogi and fish pirogi too. Small pirogis are called 'piroshki'.

When it was time to go home, he said, rather apologetically: 'Oh yes, I just remembered, well, for tomorrow's name day, I was thinking of making mushroom soup but the thing is, unfortunately I am not really very good at finding mushrooms. If you wouldn't mind... I mean, only if it's not too much trouble... you wouldn't be able to lend me a few mushrooms would you?'

'Uhuh, of course,' and I put some flat-cap and field-mushrooms, which I had recently gathered from a secret place in the wood, into a net-mesh bag for him.

Although the sun had already set, a hazy twilight still lingered, and with this and a cloudless sky as backdrop, Mr Pike, with the bag of mushrooms hanging down, slowly descended the hill.

Mr Pike setting off with his bag of mushrooms

Yan polishing the door hinges

The next day there was the type of cloudy sky that looks like it is going to rain at any moment.

I was in a gloomy mood and started to leaf through a book I had begun to read long ago, attempted to write a poem that made no sense, started to drink some tea, tried to make some buckwheat kasha,* had a go at polishing the door-hinge and wasted away the whole day.

As for Mr Pike, he didn't turn up.

* Buckwheat kasha: a Russian dish similar to risotto, made from buckwheat grain.

The following day the weather was fine. However, the air had become cooler and the wind was blowing a bit harder. I burned some dry twigs that I had collected on a small stove in the corner of the room. The little room soon warmed up and with a glad heart I set about making preparations for winter.

This day, again, there was no sign of Mr Pike.

As evening drew on, the wind died down. The twinkling light of Venus had already risen on the western horizon. I made do with a simple supper of fish soup and, intending to drink some tea, I was just boiling water in the samovar* when there came a hesitant: 'Knock, knock...' I was put in a bit of a flap and after closing the lid on the pan with the soup in it, I opened the door - keeping an eye on the sparkling hinge as I did so - and who should be standing out there but Mr Pike.

* Samovar: a Russian tea-urn. See page 41!

'Good Evening. Have you already finished supper? Oh, I am glad. The moon was shining so much I ended up going on an outing. It really is a beautiful moonlit night. A night like this could make a poet out of anybody, eh? Actually, on the way, I had a go at making up a poem myself:

I wonder if you remain aware...
That even in the midst of the severe winter chill
My river keeps on flowing silently beneath the ice.

A sleepless company on those winter evenings hide
themselves stock-still against the riverbed,
Thinking up new philosophies.

I wonder if you have seen...
How the rise in the water level
From the early spring thaw
Turns my little river into a torrent.
Creating an enormous mirror
Reflecting one cloud after another, as they drift across the deep blue sky

And I wonder if you have heard...
The sound of the river in summer
and the cries of the water fowl as they flit to and
Fro, merging one into the other.
Creating for us a moment of tranquillity.
When Summer Evening carries the scent of jasmine,
My River shows its gratitude by conveying along
a modest bouquet of cornflowers.

I wonder whether you have been touched by this...
Having been rolling autumn bilberries
in the palm of your hand
Before you know it, only one last berry is left
at the bottom of your pocket.

But as for the river-dwellers
The autumn twilight is full of sorrow.
Having done with playing their river games,
they can't return to a warm nest like you and
Unable to leave the place
Just sink back down to their solitary existence
beneath the ripples...

- Ah yes, and then there's this one:

It's the time when the mist hangs
over the evening grassland.
Caught between the has-to- begin
and has-to-come-to-an-end century,
Interwoven grass and leaves
High above my head
Cast a shadow path
To extend the universe still further

I head for that small summit and wander about.
The vision opens out wider
and from the midst of the scent of grass
drenched with dew
Comes the sound of the retreating river.
It makes exchange with my heartbeat,

A painful breath fills my heart and
Far away, where the grass lies piled up,
the whole of the River comes into view.
She vanishes into the river mist, makes a graceful curve,
then meanders here and there,
All the while leaving crescent-shaped pools bemused
behind her...
All the while, creating innumerable swamps and damp
patches of ground

Now and then, as the fancy takes her, creating a
Sheltering walnut wood and
The shade of a couple of white birch trees.
Like a sort of afterthought,
she washes the light open river banks,

Deeply, quietly, floods them with attention.
The river mullet hug the deep river-bed gloom
As the unconscious school of stonefish pass over head...

'Shall I pour you a cup of tea?' I said.

Pike reciting poetry as he takes tea with Yan

'Oh, no. I'm fine without thank you. It's already getting on, isn't it. I must be going shortly.'

Just as he was on the point of leaving, he paused, and with a very sorry-looking expression on his face, he said: 'Ah yes, tomorrow it's my name day at last but, well - after dinner at least - I thought I might want to drink some tea, but blow me if my samovar hasn't gone and broken! Uh...if you really wouldn't mind, would you be able to lend me your samovar just for the day?' 'Yes, of course,' I said and lifted up my precious samovar and handed it over to him.

Mr Pike, handling the samovar with great care and solemnity, slowly descended the evening grassland. Now and then, the moonlight reflected off the samovar and showed me where he was.

Pike with samovar

Passing through the wood and reaching the distant silver strip of the river, my samovar flashed every now and then, as it gradually moved off into the distance.

From the next day on, I saw nothing of Mr Pike.

Pike with samovar in distance,
watched from the doorway by Yan

A month later, I decided to somehow try and get down to the river myself. I put some mushroom pirogi that I had made the day before, into a bag and left the hut.

Here and there the grass on the slope had withered and frost, like crystal, clung closely to the backs of the thin long brown blades.

In the birchwood forest halfway along, the leaves had all fallen and what now stood out was the white and brown speckled bark.

The pathway was buried by fallen leaves and the sound of rustling reverberated through the midst of the woods.

The distance from my hut to the river was almost five miles at a guess. I was amazed that Mr Pike had been coming such a distance, all the way on foot.

Yan in the wood

Seeing the river close up, it was very big and I even felt a little frightened. The water flowed along calmly but in the centre of the river, small ripples rose up to the surface. The water was a slightly muddy colour and you couldn't really see through it.

The wood on the opposite bank was dense and gave off a rather gloomy feeling.

Mr Pike's hut was standing there, right before my eyes. Built on the river bank in a place that was almost within the water's reach, it was a plain hut that looked as if it had been cobbled together somehow or other from pieces of driftwood.

When I knocked on the door, which was attached to the hut by hop vines, Mr Pike popped his head out.

'Ah Yan, welcome! Hello. Well, come in right away! Make yourself at home.'

I was shown straight in to Mr Pike's hut.

The hut had been simply made but nonetheless everything inside had been kept neat and tidy. Or I should rather say, perhaps it looked like that because he didn't really have any things! Actually, speaking of 'things', there was only the samovar I had lent him on the table, the salt, butter, smetana and so on, sitting on a shelf and finally, the mushrooms, hanging up by a string.

'How about a cup of tea? I was just about to put the water on to boil in the samovar,' said Mr Pike. Then looking towards the shelf, he continued: 'Oh, that's right, I've run out of tea and sugar. Dear me! I can't even treat you to a cup of tea! How could I possibly not have noticed...' and mumbling away, he slapped himself on the forehead.

Mr Pike slapping his forehead

After that, we talked about many things for almost an hour, whilst dining on the mushroom pirogi.

I told him about how I had managed to hold out against leaks in the heavy rainstorm we had recently, and discussed ways to repair a roof.

Mr Pike spoke about the time his hut had been washed away in a flood. On that occasion apparently almost all his possessions had been destroyed.

Little by little, while we were speaking, the river mist crept in around us and began to sort of cling to my fur. The clouds began to move in a strange fashion so I decided to leave Mr Pike's house a little early.

At the doorway, he said: 'Ah yes... I'm celebrating my name day tomorrow, so please do come. I'll be making mushroom soup. Well I never! I have all the right ingredients so don't worry about a thing! But,' he continued, 'it looks as if it's going to rain, so please take my umbrella, won't you?' And he handed me a large black umbrella which had been hanging down from the eaves, already opened and ready for use.

Yan with umbrella in the rain

When you held it in your hand and looked at it from beneath, you could see that things like red rusty scraps of iron and wire had been used for the spokes and a nice-looking piece of driftwood had been chosen for the handle.

Although the fact that it was extremely heavy was a bit of a drawback, there was no doubt at all he had put a lot of effort into making it.

As I left the hut and approached the top of the bank, suddenly Mr Pike called out for me to wait a moment. 'Ah, just one thing. I beg your pardon but, if you don't mind, if it's not too inconvenient for you, would you be able to lend me just a little tea and sugar?

We have to celebrate tomorrow, you know...' he shouted out, seeming very apologetic.

'Yes, of course, I'll bring them with me tomorrow,' I said, and once more tried to look up from under the umbrella. Even if you couldn't close it, it really was very well made I thought.

The rain-swept way home was really not much fun. It was hard to climb the gentle slope as my feet kept slipping in the wet grass.

The raindrops streaming down the bark of the white birch trees soaked into the dead leaves scattered around the roots. And the rain water which had overflowed from the forest, gathered together, turning the woodland path into a small river.

I continued climbing, getting my feet soaked. Luckily, Mr Pike's umbrella didn't let the water through. But as it got wet, it became heavier and heavier.

Yellow-brown leaves, tossed down by the rain, danced fluttering here and there and stuck in my white fur. It reminded me of Mr Pike, the time before, when he had come to visit after a shower of rain with many beautiful leaves stuck to his body.

By the time I had reached my hut on the slope of the hill, it was turning into a heavy downpour.

That evening there was a flood.

The next day, the rain had let up but the sky was as changeable as ever. The air, heavy with dampness, clung to the body and it wasn't a very nice feeling. But today was Mr Pike's name day, so despite the weather, I descended the slope in rather a cheerful mood, carrying a bag of sugar and a box of tea.

Just as Mr Pike had described on another occasion, many different kinds of clouds were drifting about in the huge expanse of sky spread out before me.

Yan walking to Pike's house, with his box of tea

Above the hill, there was one cloud which looked as if it were touching the ground. As I went down the hillside, it gradually rose higher and higher above my head, until it had disappeared into the distance. Then there was another cloud dancing wildly this way and that, so that before you knew it, it had travelled from east to west, where it turned into a neat line and ended up floating away.

The river had become completely muddy and flowed along with its shoulders squared right up against the riverbank. I carried the tea and sugar carefully so that they didn't get wet and sat down on the grass.

After a while of sitting dreamily, watching the river flow by, I noticed some sort of shining thing on the slightly elevated slope further upstream.

I walked towards the upper stream, running alongside the bank, and compared to its surroundings, the grasses looked even taller.

Right in the middle of that grassland, my samovar stood glittering.

The sky had completely brightened up and the sunlight poured down on me, and on the samovar, with all its might.

Samovar in the grassland

I drew up some spring water from alongside the riverbank, boiled some tea in the samovar and drank it. I let my mind wander off, and for half a day, I waited for Mr Pike to make an appearance.

In the end, Mr Pike didn't turn up.

Carrying the samovar, I turned back along the path. Perhaps because of the weight of the samovar, the journey home seemed to drag on and on. In the midst of yesterday's flood, Mr Pike must have carried my samovar up to the highest ground... his home may have been washed away... along with the ingredients for the mushroom soup...

Thinking about how we wouldn't be able to celebrate his name day after all, I climbed up the hillside.

As I arrived at the hut, Mr Pike's umbrella, which I had put outside as I was on my way out, was already completely dry.

Yan and the Samovar

Yan wrapped in blankets

*   *   *

Before you know it, two months have passed.

Wrapped up in a blanket, I whiled away the winter day by day, little by little, burning the twigs that I had gathered and put aside over the autumn.

The clear winter days were a wonderful sight. Both the grassland and the woods became white all over with absolutely nothing left in sight to dirty this world. Snow lay as far as the distant horizon, and wiped away all trace of the flowing river there.

In the struggle of day to day living, I had completely forgotten about Mr Pike.

*   *   *

*　　　*　　　*

At this point in the story, Spring suddenly arrives.

And then one day, unexpectedly, Summer too has come to an end.

Golden Autumn has come around once again.

*　　　*　　　*

It had stopped raining, and with an azure sky above me and a basket made from white birch bark hanging down by my side, I was on my way to a secret wood to do some mushroom-picking.

In the middle of the wood, there was still an echo of summer and just the right humid conditions for the mushrooms to grow. Chestnut mushrooms, 'straw-hat' mushrooms, 'broomstick' mushrooms... whatever type of mushroom you care to name, I could pick a basketful of it.

With great satisfaction, I came out of the wood and just as I was approaching the grassland, I remembered about the mushroom soup and about the fact that Mr Pike hadn't been able to make any.

I followed the path around to the left and headed for the river.

Yan returns through the woods
from mushroom-picking

Yan with the bag of mushrooms
in a field of starflowers

I cut across the field of starflowers, taking care not to trample on them, and having passed through a thicket of flowering shrubs with small white cross-shaped flowers, I came out where the river was flowing smoothly by.

A few waves were rising up in the middle of the river and little fishes were having fun splashing around. I watched dreamily, as the faded green leaves began drifting downstream. And little by little, the leaves that had not yet fallen were beginning to turn.

The wood on the opposite bank was hidden in the rising river mist.

Mr Pike swimming in the river

'What a surprise! Yan! What on earth are you doing here? Hello there! It's really fine weather we're having today, isn't it? A day like today would give anyone the urge to go on an outing. I was just thinking about going out somewhere myself.'

And that was how I ended up chatting to Mr Pike again after such a long time. I showed him how to tell if a mushroom is poisonous and how to make a beautiful replica lace-curtain using leaves from a tree. Mr Pike told me about the place where watercress grew and where to find a secret spring that had delicious water gushing out from it.

'By the way, your house used to be somewhere near hear, I thought...'

'Ah, yes, it was over there somewhere, but it was washed away in this last flood we had. Talking of which, my feelings were also swept a good way down-river! It was really fun riding with the flow, but coming back upstream again was very hard-going.'

'When you say 'this last flood we had', do you mean the flood that happened last autumn?'

'Yes, that's right, that's the one I mean.'

Having chatted for just under an hour, the two of us sort of ran out of things to say. There was the sound of the river rushing by, with some little fish splashing in and out of the water. Now and then, the leaves of the shrub behind me rustled in the breeze that came from the opposite bank.

With a sky the colour of lapis lazuli in the background, before you knew it, a faint red colour had spread out over the surface of the river.

When I mentioned that it was time for me to be heading home, Mr Pike saw me off as far as the top of the bank. At our parting, after I had shared out the mushrooms that I had picked that day with him, he said:

'Ah yes, that reminds me, tomorrow I am celebrating my name day. I'll be making mushroom soup so please do come.'

'Of course I'll come,' I said, and went through the shrub blossoming with the small white cross-shaped flowers.

Mr Pike waving goodbye from the riverbank

Yan looking back at him

Just as I was coming out on the other side, onto the path in the grassy shade, Mr Pike added, as usual, calling out in a loud voice:

'Ah, one more thing, I just remembered, but, if it's not too much trouble, I've just gone and run out of butter and salt so, if you don't mind... if you're sure you don't mind that is, would you be able to lend me a little bit?'

'Right ho, I'll be sure to bring some with me tomorrow,' I shouted back.

Then I cut across the field of starflowers, to the wood where the mushrooms grew, and from there I followed the path as it curved towards the grassy slope of the hill.

Step by step, as I climbed through the grass, my heart gradually filled with an inexpressible feeling of happiness.

I looked back the way I had come, to see it shrouded already in darkness. And there, in the far distance, a strip of silver was shining, gently.

Afterword

If for homework you were asked to write a composition about what you have just read, you would probably feel a bit irritated and say something like
'What a bother. What's the point?'

If you are of the opinion that when it comes to your impressions of, say, a book, or a film or a piece of music, it's enough to leave them vaguely drifting around inside your head, you might end up writing something like:

'The story is set in Russia. Although having said that, Russia is never actually mentioned. In fact, if you think of it being about a place with plenty of wide open space and a certain amount of nature left, it could be set just about anywhere.

One day, a cat called Yan is paid an unexpected visit by a pike. He has never met this pike before in his life. But in honour of the pike's ever-anticipated name day, Yan gives him the ingredients to make mushroom soup and even lends him his precious samovar too. Yan has absolutely no worries in doing this... and likewise the pike has no qualms about asking for them.

The type of friendship they experience with each other is open, and trusting. They form a close bond through their physical encounters both with each other, and with the world that they share. Speaking of their world, I think the world written about by Chekhov in 'The Steppe' may have been the same. The characters are tiny figures amid the vast grassland plains known as The Steppe.

A year after their first meeting, the Pike again asks Yan to lend him some butter and salt. Yan seems to be happy with the easy way in which the Pike asks for things, without feeling apologetic about the fact that he is always asking, or indeed without even thinking too much about it. There is a sense of an abundant and limitless kindness that allows them to trust in nature and accept everything with ease.'

Well, it is not up to me whether you get an 'excellent', a 'very good' or a Grade A. Basically, each reader will have their own impression and no two will be the same. Moreover, unfortunately you can't find much of a theme in this story. It is just about these two people - I mean, two animals - drinking tea, chatting, reciting poems and so on. Every day passes by without event. Actually no, it doesn't exactly 'pass by'. The fact that the arrival of the pike's name day is always put off until tomorrow keeps you permanently caught up in their grassland world. So that even when you have come to the end of this rather short story, you will still be wandering about somewhere between the big river where the pike lives and the place on the hillside, where Yan has his home.

You will have no idea where you are going. But it is an important thing to be in that situation. Try taking a stroll there, without any reason or particular aim. You might cut your hand on the long thin grass, or prick yourself on the thorns of the thistles. Try looking up at the starflowers, swaying before your eyes as you lie down in the midst of them. Press your foot into the mud, or stand on the riverbank and stare dreamily into the surface of the water. Try stepping on the fallen leaves, your shoes getting wet from the water that oozes out. Take a stealthy peep at that river from behind a bush of the shrub whose name you don't know. Then climb the hillside and look at the river, glittering in the distance. If you do this, you may end up looking at that river and at that pike with the same eyes as Yan.

A word after the afterword (P.P.S)

If you are of the opinion that the pike is being sneaky - by always borrowing things and never returning them - that proves you are rather tired. Please take the day off. You have my permission to be absent from school and there's no need to do any homework. In fact, while I mention it, you don't have to go to the office either. Just laze away the whole day in blissful idleness.

If it occurs to you that the pike might be using his name day as an excuse - throw a toothbrush into your bag and hand in your resignation immediately. Take a trip... anywhere you like. It's up to you if you choose to roam around strange and distant lands, a cheap hotel at each destination, spending your life in this way, with nothing left at the end of it. Except the toothbrush.

And for those of you who feel that you simply can't do that, and that you absolutely have to go on with the routine of daily life, you may take some comfort in making this mushroom soup, which the pike - in all probability - never got to taste.

Mushroom Soup

If you can't get hold of ceps, use the mushroom of your choice, such as shitake or button mushrooms. Cut them into small pieces and cook in vegetable stock. Melt plenty of butter in a frying pan, fry some chopped onions and finely diced carrot, and add to the mushrooms. Then chop some potato into small pieces and add this in as well. Add some fine pasta and season with salt. At the table, garnish with a generous dollop of smetana (if no smetana, use a little sour cream) and there you go! - it's ready to eat!

(From the kitchen of Ekatherina Tribelskaia and Mariko Machida)

If you are interested in taking this further, you may like to refer to chapter 16 of Russian Exile Food, co-authored by Peter Vail and Alexander Genis.

And another word after that! (P.P.P.S)

The writing of this short picture book has its beginnings in a poem called "Cape Cod Lullaby" by the Russian exiled poet Joseph Brodsky:

The door creaks.
Standing in the doorway there is a cod.

The cod begs for a drink.
Yes of course, in the name of God.

The traveller probably could do with a slice of bread too
And I teach him the way to go. It is a winding path.
The fish takes his leave.

But no sooner has he left...

When another fish, again, knocks at the door.

And in this way, a school of fish is formed, passing through my house the whole night long.

(From Numano Mitsuyoshi's A Stop Before Eternity Station, Sakuhinsha Publications, 1989)

I quote this not for the noble reason of having being enlightened by this extract from a metaphysical poem.

It was just that, in the bit when the door opens and there's the face of a cod out there (I felt from the first that the idea of a cod with a face was a bit over the top) I thought it was a bit scary, but that it might be interesting if it were a pike. However, when one cod shows up after another, all looking the same, appearing to form a school (cod swim in schools, you see) and as it all happens in a place called 'Cape Cod', it would have to be a cod.

But how would the face of a pike look? For a long time I began to think about it and a vague image of a pike's face, long but well-proportioned in its own way, came to mind.

I wasn't sure where that type of image came from - but no doubt the pike drawn on the small box by Pareq and the drawing of one from the folk tale by Omelia were somewhere in the back of my mind. And blow me down if these, reinforced by the rather scientific ink drawings of pike in Aksakov's 'Miscellaneous Fishing Tales' (1986 Kyobunsha publications - in which book you can find a description of the catching of a 267 year old pike) weren't the beginning of all my misguided impressions.

When I was faced with sea-pike on display at the supermarket and the fishmongers, I had plenty of opportunity to observe them.

At any rate, as it is the same pike whether it comes from the river or the sea, I expected it's basic body shape to be the same. The shock came when, a short time after I'd finished drawing all the pictures, I came across a book of Russian recipes published in America. In it was a picture of a pike lying like a log, resplendent amongst all these other ingredients. And although its face was certainly long, its mouth was rounded like the toe of a boot. So please, dear reader - and I swear on the Pike's honour - please don't think that his mouth is as pointed as I've made it look in my pictures. Although most Japanese fish are flatfish, a great many foreign fish are of the full-bodied variety. This is because our cultures have diverged, ours (think of our dry fish) is a culture of cutting open, whilst abroad they have a culture of stuffing (over there, they serve stuffed fish just like stuffed quail). As soon as it is ready to serve, Japanese fish are placed on their side, but overseas, the fish is placed on its belly and served in the upright position. For which reason, thinking things out in 3-dimensions is our weak point. And that is how, with my flat perspective of the pike, I made a big mistake. Please note that the shape of a real pike is completely different from what I have drawn.

I know I went off the track a bit when I was writing the last paragraph. It's just that I felt I was with Yan, climbing up the slope of the grassland, step by step and, even though I was writing it myself, tears were welling up in my eyes.

How many times have I found myself coming and going between that river and that hill, knowing where each thing is to be found, how the path turns, where there is a good view. I have made accurate copies in the map of my mind.

I think it was the fact that I knew I would probably not be walking along this path again and the sense that I would have to leave the land of Yan and the Pike that made me feel the way I did.

Well, the time has come for me to hand this small work over to Yan and to you, the reader. Unfortunately, I don't know the whereabouts of the Pike, so I can't hand it over to him!

To Mariko Machida - the first person to read this book, my critic, my researcher about food from a country little known to our own and a woman who made up for my poor lack of knowledge - my admiration and gratitude.

Translator's Acknowledgements:
To Chiaki Yamase and Reiko Iwata
for liasing with Mr Machida, and to
Yoko Shinohara who takes care of me
whenever I go to Japan.

the acorn book of *contemporary* haiku
Edited by Lucien Stryk and Kevin Bailey

Bringing together the work of over 140 poets from
25 countries, this anthology is the most comprehensive
collection of international haiku to be published in the UK.

Edited by Lucien Stryk (*Penguin Book of Zen Poetry,
the Haiku of Bashō*) and Kevin Bailey (*HQ magazine*).

From the traditional to the experimental,
this collection of over four hundred poems, provides the perfect
introduction to this exciting and developing form.

'An excellent anthology ... plenty for readers to savour for a
long time.' - *NH International*

£6.99   ISBN 0 9534205 2 3

only when the sun shines brightly
by Magnus Mills

Magnus Mills caught the limelight when he became the first
bus driver to be short-listed for the Booker Prize.
His novel: 'The Restraint of Beasts' went on to sell over
30,000 copies and has been translated into 16 languages.
This is his first collection of short stories.

'Each one a gem.' - *Time Out*

'Beautifully produced.' - *The Daily Telegraph*

£3.99 ISBN 0 9534205 1 5

---

water
by Chris Mulhern

A haiku journey, each section corresponding to one aspect
of water - from snowmelt and cloud water to dry land.

water:
your seeking for dryness, for thirst
for all that is arid in me

'A book to be explored, to lose yourself in.' - *Presence Magazine*

'Filled with fine things.' - *Lucien Stryk*

£4.99 ISBN 0 9534205 0 7

All titles are available direct from

acorn book company
PO Box 191, Tadworth
Surrey KT20 5YQ

POST FREE IN THE UK

Cheques payable to acorn book company.
or email your order to sales@acornbook.co.uk

acorn book company

is an independent
publisher of small, high quality editions.

We also operate a mail order web-site.

For more information
please visit us at:
www.acornbook.co.uk